Lizbeth Lou
Got a Rock in Her Shoe

written by Troy Howell

illustrated by Kathryn Carr

Lizbeth Lou got a rock in her shoe.

"Ow!" Lizzy said. "This just will not do!"
She flung it, it crashed . . .

in a cricket's canoe.

"Whoa!" said the cricket. "A boulder—I'm sunk!"
He dumped it, it dropped . . .

on a trout with a clunk.
"Ugh!" said the trout. "This is too tough to chew!"

He spat it, it soared . . .

toward a duck's good-as-new flowered
umbrella she'd brought to the zoo.

"A raindrop!" she said. "But it's solid as lead!"

She pitched it, it sped . . .

past a worker ant's head.

"My!" said the ant. "My goodness—a pill!
As big as a boxcar, as big as a hill!"

She rolled it, and rolled it,

and rolled it until . . .

it stuck in the sidewalk,
just stuck, wouldn't move.
Along came a bike and
it lodged in a groove.

Around and around the pebble did spin,
till it shot from the tire—
went higher and higher . . .

and higher, to rest
on a woman's hatpin.

A bird saw it there, thinking it was a seed,
and dove down to get it . . .

He tucked it away in his gentleman's coat,
which had a small hole, as small as a mote,
down at the bottom, like a footnote.*

*A footnote is a small explanation at
the bottom of the page, like this.

but it had been freed
by a gentleman friend, who'd picked it with care,
not wanting the woman to know it was there.

Out the rock came, right back in the game
of "what goes around comes around"—
you'd think it took aim.

For it ended up tumbling along in the grass,
joggling and toggling and making a dash
toward a girl named Lizbeth, as she went past.
Who, you may ask, Lizbeth who?

Lizbeth Lou said, "This just will not do!"

First Edition 2016
Library of Congress Control Number 2015953406
ISBN 978-0-9913866-5-9

1 2 3 4 5 6 7 8 9 10
Printed in Malaysia

This book was typeset in Minion Pro.
The illustrations are hand-cut paper silhouettes arranged,
illuminated, and photographed in dioramas.
Book design by Kathryn Carr and Amanda Broder

Ripple Grove
Press
Portland, OR
www.RippleGrovePress.com

To my friends in Richmond Children's Writers,
who were there when the rock began to roll—T. H.

To my mother, who first introduced me to
children's books—K. C.

Ripple Grove
Press